I0543968

www.ChloeEmile.com

Annie's Story

Brides of Fall River

CHLOE EMILE

ISBN-13: 978-1987859256
ISBN-10: 1987859251

CONTENTS

CHAPTER ONE

1800s, *Fall River, Massachusetts*

I was christened Anna Margarete Lochlan, but everyone always called me Annie. I grew up on our family farm in Fall River, Massachusetts with my two sisters and twin brothers. My sisters and I were part of a set of fraternal triplets.

When I close my eyes, I can still feel my childhood as though it were only yesterday, yet I know that is not the case. Many years have passed since those early days when we were all on the farm.

I recall how much I loved the piano. I wanted to learn how to play it. Mama had arranged for Agatha Sullivan to teach me how to play, and in return, I would help Miss Agatha with her canning for the season. The Sullivan farm was north of ours and a bit bigger. Miss Agatha had six sons, all single, and they worked the farm. Since their father had passed, the winter before I started my lessons, the boys had run the farm for their mother.

I knew the youngest son, Travis. He was in my class at school for a short time before he left to work on the farm full-time. I remember when I first saw him—his sandy blond hair and those green eyes that seemed to hypnotize me when he looked at me. He was the only one in the family with that eye color. He was handsome, but like me, he was shy.

When we were still in school together, every Wednesday after school I'd walk to Miss Agatha's, and Travis would come with me. We would talk about classes or homework assignments. It made the long walk seem shorter, and I always looked forward to Wednesdays.

We came out of our shells when we were alone together, although the shyness was still there. Now, looking back, I realize we probably liked each other and didn't know how to express it.

At the Sullivans' house, Miss Agatha taught me piano for an hour, and I helped with canning for half an hour after that. I loved the piano, and Miss Agatha said I was getting very good at it. Life then seemed simple and good. I never thought it would all come to a crashing end, but it did.

The news came fast: on April 12, 1861, Fort Sumter was fired on, and two days later, the Rebel flag was flying over the fort. Men and young boys were answering the call. Seventy-five thousand men joined the union army.

The three older Sullivan boys went the first week. A grand total of 146,000 men from Massachusetts joined the cause and rallied for the nation. Each day, news of the battles would come to the telegraph office, letting us know what was happening and what battles were being fought.

Around the time the three older Sullivan brothers went off to war, the younger three, including Travis, had to drop out of school to take care of the farm. To help the cause, Mama and the other ladies kept themselves busy with sewing. Charity functions raised money to help the families of those brave men who were killed in the battles.

At one of the charity balls, when we were both fourteen, I saw Travis standing by the wall, looking glum and not asking any girls to dance. I wasn't talkative. My sisters were the chatty ones. I had spent most of the night in the field next to the barn where the ball was held, watching the night sky. I always loved the night sky. Something about the moon and the stars just fascinated me. I preferred it to a busy party.

Travis left early. He came out of the barn and had started down past the field when he noticed me. He thought I'd fallen and needed help, so he rushed over. "Are you all right?"

I looked up into his beautiful green eyes. They were hypnotizing, and I had to quickly snap out of it. "Yes. Why are you asking such a foolish question?"

"Well, ma'am, I saw you on the ground and..."

I must have looked strange, staring at the stars. I smiled and started to laugh. "Maybe I should explain." I sat up. "I was looking up at the night sky. Ever since I was a little girl, my mother would tell us about the gypsy dancing in the moonlight." By the look on his face, I could tell I had confused him. "It was a story told to her by her mother. We had the gypsy story from Mama, and from my father, I had story of the wee folk."

"The wee folk?"

"Papa came from Ireland, and they have the little people who come out at..." I looked at him and decided not to describe the story any further. "I'll just leave it at that. I just love looking at the night sky."

10

"So do I. I mean, the stars are always twinkling. They look like diamonds up there."

I looked up and then back to him again. "You're right. I never thought of them that way. They do look like diamonds."

I started to smile.

His eyes crinkled when he smiled back. "You have a nice smile, ma'am."

"So do you."

"Would you like to have me walk you home? It's not far out of my way."

"That would be very nice."

We started down the road side by side. It felt like old times. It had been a few years since he'd been in school. We walked and talked probably more than he'd done with anyone in his life. Travis had always been quiet. I rarely saw him talk to any other girls for very long.

Unfortunately, after that, I didn't get a chance to talk at length with him for almost ten years. It took a young boy inadvertently playing cupid to bring us together again.

CHAPTER TWO

The four years of war were long. Sometimes we would see a soldier walking up the road, going home, wherever that was. They were tired and hungry. All they wanted was to be back home with their families. We tried to do all we could.

My mama was a great person. She had a way of making everyone feel welcome. There wasn't a soldier who passed by our road whom she didn't offer a smile, a place to rest from their journey, and food. She treated them with kindness and respect since, after all, they were the returning heroes. But some of those young men never came back. Some of the ones who lived had lost their minds.

Papa had thought about joining, but Mama convinced him otherwise. They didn't have arguments but rather "discussions," as Mama called them. My brothers were too young to join, and for that, we were all glad.

The war finally ended, and life slowly came back to normal. Unfortunately, at the end of the war, Agatha Sullivan passed away. Even after all these years, I still miss her pleasant voice and the way she played the piano. She was like the grandmother I never had. I've always remembered her advice and have followed it many times in my life. She told me that I was confident and capable and that I had a lot to offer the world.

Of the triplets, I had always been the quieter, more sensitive one. As I grew into my teenage years, I began to realize I was not like my sisters and didn't need to be. I was my own person. Mama would tell me that we all had different goals in life and they should reflect what we wanted, not what others had chosen for us.

I took this advice to heart too. The day I decided to be a teacher was one of the happiest of my life. I was all of twenty-two years old and felt I wanted to give something to the children of Fall River. We had just lived through a war that had divided the nation, and it had had a devastating effect on all of us. I just wanted to give the children a sense of stability, love, and care as the nation started to heal its wounds.

Our grandpa had left everyone enough money to live comfortably for the rest of our lives, but there wasn't any reason I couldn't do more and give back to society. This was my chance to give the children something that would benefit them for the rest of their lives: an education.

The last teacher at the school had left to marry her fiancé, who had come home from the war. She had gone back to New York with him to settle down and start her own family as so many of the teachers did. It was a good chance for me to apply for the job.

Mama also seemed to think it was a good idea. It would be a service to the town as well as a way for me to open new avenues. With newer settlers coming into the town each day, it was clear that Fall River was growing, and there was a need for a teacher. The town board interviewed me for the position. Even though there were no other candidates, they still required an interview and a vote.

On my first day as the new teacher, I was as excited as the students. I expected to see many eager faces, and I was right. Young boys and girls who wanted to learn about life outside of

Fall River, far from where the train stopped, came into my classroom.

Many of them were new to Fall River, and there were also the children of farmers and storekeepers, who didn't attend often. I had a well-rounded mixture of town and rural children. As they all found desks to sit at, I smiled at them.

"Good morning, class. My name is Annie Lochlan, but you can call me Miss Annie. That will make it easy. Now, I don't know about you, but I like it when things are easy."

They all seemed to agree on that one. I learned each of their names and a little about themselves. One of the most touching moments was when Cal Sullivan walked up to me and placed a little white puppy in my arms.

"Miss Annie, here's is a pup from my pa's prize hunting dog's litter. She'll make you a good house dog. I hope you like her, ma'am."

I looked at the dog, and it was love at first sight. She was a soft ball of fluff and so small, and she needed a name. What a perfect project for the students. I smiled at Cal then handed the puppy back to him.

"Cal, I need your help to hold her for a bit, okay?"

A smile came to the boy's face. "Yes, Miss Annie."

Cal was Travis's nephew. His grandma was the same Mrs. Agatha Sullivan who'd taught me how to play the piano. Cal's family also lived on a farm, not far from his uncle Travis's farm. I hadn't seen Cal's pa, Ethan, since the war. I didn't even remember the last time I'd seen Travis. He was rarely in town.

Cal was the only child of the oldest Sullivan son to actually go to school—not meaning any disrespect to the boys. They all knew how to read and write. Miss Agatha had made sure of that, God rest her soul. But book learning was something they never seemed to have time for. Their farm was bigger than ours, and Cal's father needed his boys in the fields helping instead of in school. The pup was a thoughtful gift since she was from Cal's pa's prize dog. I looked up at the class.

"Now, I would like your help on a very special project, class. Cal, here, has graciously given me a puppy. In case you are thinking of the same gift, I must warn you my mother only allows one pet per family. Since our pup will be coming to school each day, she will need a name. So, your first assignment is to think of a name for her. This will be your homework assignment for tonight, but for now, let's see how far you are in your schoolwork. Let's start with history. Take out your history books. Turn to Chapter Five. Martha, would you like to start reading at the top of the page?"

As Martha read, I walked around the room to see how the others were keeping up with the reading. Many of the older ones were doing fine, but I did see I would need to change the reading schedules for the lower grades.

Many of the younger ones needed readers for below their grades. I was sure there was one in the study at home, and I would have to check and see if there were any at the school.

The older children seemed to be following the text, but then again, it was the first day back from summer vacation, and they still had dreams of running outside. Didn't blame them. I would too if I was their age.

As I walked into the house that afternoon, Mama took one look at the puppy and shook her head. "Annie, I thought you outgrew bringing strays home."

"Oh, Mama, she's not a stray. She's a gift from Cal Sullivan. Isn't she pretty?"

Papa came in and saw the pup, too. "Annie, you know what this dog is, don't you?"

"Sure. Cal said she was from his father's prize hunting dog's litter."

"Prize or no prize, what you have there is a wolf pup."

"Oh, Papa, don't be silly. She's not a wolf. Look at her..."

"It's a wolf. I've seen enough to know the difference. Besides, Ethan Sullivan has hounds for hunting, not this kind of dog."

I looked at the dog then back at my father. "But why would Cal lie to me?"

"Honey, he knew it was safe with you. Most likely, judging by the size of the little one, she's not too old—five or six weeks old. I figure Ethan killed her mama and, well, maybe he would do the same to her if Cal didn't take her to you. The boy saved her life."

"Well, I'm keeping her, Papa. You'll see. She'll be fine, and no one will know she's not a puppy."

I went upstairs and didn't come down for supper that night. I was looking out the window at the night sky, and I didn't even hear Mama walk into the room. I turned around, and she was there.

"I knocked, but you didn't hear me."

"I'm sorry, Mama, but I'm not letting Ethan Sullivan kill this poor creature for no reason."

"Annie, you do know that is a wild animal."

"She's a pup, and with the right environment and love, she can be tamed." I wanted so much for her to understand.

She smiled at the pup. "She's very cute and so soft."

"See, Mama—she's just a baby. She hasn't learned to be bad, and I won't teach her to be."

"All right Annie. We'll give it a try. But if there is a problem, she goes. Is that understood?"

"Yes, Mama. Thank you, Mama."

Mama gave me a final hug and left.

The following afternoon, Ethan Sullivan paid a visit to the farm. He had come to see me, but I was not home from school yet, so Papa spoke to him. I heard the story later.

"I can appreciate your concern," Papa had told Ethan, "but Annie is set on raising the pup. I told her as long as there is no problem, she can raise her."

"You don't understand," Ethan said. "It's a wild animal."

"Yes, I know, and I explained that to Annie, but she's dead set on proving me wrong."

"I know the feeling." Ethan sighed. "I have a ten-year-old son who wants to save every animal in the world."

"I have it here also. Annie always took in every stray. Why, she even had a cougar cub once. She cried for a week when I told her she couldn't let it sleep in the house."

"Just remember, once that pup grows, it's gonna draw every male wolf to your door."

"I'll worry about that when the time comes."

Ethan was gone before I got home that day. Oh, yes—Papa told me the whole story, but I was set on keeping the puppy. Ethan would only kill her before she got a chance to grow up.

It was pretty quiet at the supper table. Mama asked how school was, and I only answered briefly. I did tell her the class had agreed on a name for the pup. She was to be named Chance, meaning she had a second chance.

Papa turned to me. "Annie, you're set on going through with this, but you can't take the pup to school with all those children. When their folks see her, they're gonna know she's not a dog. Their folks won't allow a wolf in the same room with their children. You have to see their point on this."

"I suppose so, but that don't change a thing, Papa. I'm gonna prove you and Mr. Sullivan wrong."

The air was warm as I sat in the rose garden later in the evening. I loved to go out there. I'd sit there and talk things out in my mind. Lordy, I would sit out there for hours like that. It was almost like going to church, maybe because of the cemetery just up from the garden, and I always felt that if I prayed there, God would hear me.

I always made sure I said a prayer for all those up there and ask them if they could send a good word on my behalf. There were times I even thought I would hear the answer clearly as if someone were out there with me. I never told anyone about that or the fact that I'd seen faces in the bark of the trees.

Papa always said the wee folk were around, too, keeping watch over the young ones. As a child, I used to look around at night for them. I never did see one.

I was still looking up at the night sky when Mama walked over to me. "Watching the gypsy dancing in the moonlight?"

I looked at her and smiled. "Oh, Mama, you used to tell us that story when we were kids. When I was younger, I would sit and look out my window at the moon, trying to find the gypsy. I was always disappointed that I never could find her. It was like Papa's wee folk. I never found them either."

"And I'm gonna keep telling that story. After all, I have grandchildren to pass it down to, and one day, I'd like to see a grandchild from you or maybe two."

"Well, when I'm ready, you can tell my children about the gypsy."

I saw the surprised look on her face. "Are you...?"

"No, Mama, not just yet. There is no one I have an interest in now, so there is no need to bring out the shoes and rice just yet. Besides, the way you talk, one would think you're trying to get rid of me. Are you trying to get rid of me?"

"Oh, of course not. You tell me when you're ready. I'm going to leave you out here. Your papa will be snacking on the cake I made for the church social tomorrow night, and there will be nothing left before too long. You know how your father gets with chocolate cake."

I laughed. She got up and headed for the back door.

"Good night, Mama."

Mama didn't understand why I wasn't ready to settle down just yet. I thought I was still young. I didn't feel the pressure to get married although I did miss my sisters.

I looked up at the moon and smiled. "Oh, you crazy gypsy. You're dancing up there tonight. Could it be that you're trying to tell me something? Can you hear me? Maybe your magic will come my way. Maybe you'll come and visit me in my dreams. Show me what's ahead in my life—or maybe I don't want to see it. Oh, but then again, a small hint would be nice."

Maybe talking to the moon was a little crazy, but it comforted me. I didn't know what my life was going to be like, but it was nice to dream about. Mama was a bit worried about me—I knew that.

My sisters were married, and there I was, still single at an age when many women were happily married and raising families. Oh, the idea had come to mind a few times, but there were a few things that would have to be considered. I took one more look at the moon and smiled. "*You keep dancing, gypsy.*"

CHAPTER THREE

In the following weeks, Chance grew. She became a bit too big to fit in my lap although she didn't see it that way. Despite what Papa warned about, she still was gentle, even when walking in the backyard.

Chance never strayed from my side. The wolf was perfectly tame, except on one afternoon. I was sitting on the front porch one day when Ethan Sullivan came riding up. I actually saw the hair on Chance's back stand up straight and she let out a low, guttural growl.

Though Chance didn't leave my side, she still never took her eyes off Mr. Sullivan. Papa had Mr. Sullivan go inside, but Chance kept looking at the door. For some reason, Chance had a bad memory of Ethan Sullivan. When he came back out, he gave me and Chance a stony look then got on his horse and rode off.

Papa had a worried expression on his face when he came over to me. "Annie, where was Chance last night?"

"What, Papa?"

"Was Chance in your room all night?"

"Of course. Where else would she be? She never leaves the house without me. What's this all about?"

"Well, seems Ethan Sullivan lost one of his sheep last night. The poor thing was torn apart, and the only animal that could do that kind of damage was a wolf."

I looked at Chance and knew she couldn't do it. There was no way she could have jumped out the window and fallen from the top floor and still been able to walk. Besides, how would she have been able to get back inside again?

"No, Papa. Chance would never do a thing like that. Why, she's gentle with all the critters around here. She's been here for three weeks now, and never given us any trouble. If she had gotten out, she wouldn't have been able to climb back in. You have the wrong wolf. Just 'cause she's a wolf doesn't this mean she's responsible for every animal that's killed in this town. Besides, wolves aren't the only animals that attack sheep. You also have cougars that roam at night."

The expression on his face told me that he was thinking the same thing.

The next morning, I came downstairs in a hurry to get to work. I left Chance in my room with the door locked so there would be no question where she would be all day. Mama looked at me as I headed for the door.

"Annie, don't be so hard on your father. He had to ask."

"How could you both think Chance could do such a thing? I told you she was in my room all night."

"I know you love the animal, but the fact is she's a wild creature, and how can you be sure she's with you all night long?"

"Maybe Ethan Sullivan just wants her dead like her ma, and Chance knows that."

"Come on now—how can she know that?"

"Humans have a scent to them. You taught us that when we were young. That's why we didn't take the babies from the mamas when they were little. Once the mama got the scent of a human on her baby, she wouldn't feed it. Well, Ethan Sullivan's scent triggers a memory for Chance. I think it's 'cause he killed her mama."

I could see that it was no use trying to get through to Mama, so I left. We never spoke of it again until three weeks later, when Ethan Sullivan came back with another gentleman. It seems they were looking for Papa. Mama had them sit in the living room and wait while she got Papa. I tried to sneak upstairs but Papa stopped me.

"Annie, can you come in here? Leave Chance there in the hall."

"Why?"

"Because I asked you to."

I went into the living room. Chance wanted to follow, but I told her to stay, and I closed the door. I turned to meet the stares of Mr. Sullivan and the other man.

"What's this all about, Papa?" I asked.

"Well, Annie, this here is Mr. Henry Hunter. He lives close to Mr. Sullivan on the northern side."

I smiled at him politely. I remembered him from the time I would go to Mrs. Sullivan's for piano lessons.

Papa continued. "Seems his sheep were scattered around last night, and one of his hands saw the wolf that was chasing them."

I turned to Mr. Hunter. "And Mr. Hunter, you are here to tell me that it's my wolf. Am I correct?"

"Well, Miss, it seems your wolf fits the description."

"Papa, open the door. I want Mr. Hunter to see Chance up close. I want him to make sure this is the wolf his hands described."

When the door opened, Chance was still sitting there.

"Chance, come!"

The animal slowly made her way toward me. I bent down on one knee to greet her. "You see, gentlemen, she's not a killer. If you'd like, you can come closer to her and decide for yourselves. Or if you like, I can get a few of our chickens to run around the room here, and you'll see she's not interested."

"But Miss, you have to admit having a wolf as a pet is... well, it's a bit out of the ordinary," Mr. Hunter said.

"As you can see, Chance behaves like any other domesticated animal, but I do admit she can look rather terrifying to someone who doesn't know she's tame."

Ethan Sullivan was not convinced. As he stepped closer to Chance, the dog gave a low growl.

"You see—that's not a tame animal. That's a wild beast."

I wasn't going to let him win. "This is the second time she's growled at you, Mr. Sullivan. Mr. Hunter, would you be so kind as to step forward? I have a theory. I promise I won't let anything happen to you."

"Well, if you promise, Miss..."

He took two to three steps, and Chance just sat there, not making a sound.

"That doesn't prove anything," Mr. Sullivan exclaimed. "The dog doesn't like me."

"I agree with you, Mr. Sullivan. I wonder why she doesn't like you. Could it be because you killed her mother?"

"That's ridiculous. How could a—"

I explained that Chance knew him by scent. "They know when they're looking at an enemy and when it's a person who won't harm them. Now, this is just a guess on my part, but you seem to trigger an unpleasant memory for her. I'm thinking she's remembering when you killed her mama."

That prompted Ethan's mood to drop. He lashed out at me. "You don't know what you are talking about. Everybody knows you're the crazy one of the sisters. There's been talk around town for years. I remember when you were a young girl and would come to have my mother teach you how to play the piano. Lord, how I would dread Wednesday afternoons. It meant I would have to suffer hearing you banging on those keys. My mother would smile and tell you that you were improving, but Lord, there was no improvement. You just got worse with each lesson. You always kept to yourself. I mean, look at your sisters. They are all married to fine gentlemen, and here you are. You should be married with youngins of your own, and you're playing mama to a wolf pup. Why, people say they see you walking in the woods, talking to yourself. That's not normal. You're not normal. Maybe that's why you're never in town. You're a freak."

Papa glowered at him as if he would shoot him. "Mr. Sullivan, I would like you to leave my home."

"Look, you can cover up all you want, Ryan, but everyone knows your girl is not right. I tell you I wouldn't trust her teaching my son.

She'd be filling his head with all kinds of crazy ideas—that he can be better than a farmer or that he can go to college."

"What's so crazy about telling the boy he can have something better than the life he knows?" Papa demanded.

"You're getting like your daughter now, Ryan. You can't mean to say it's right to fill a boy's mind with fool notions and not practical schooling."

What happened next was hard for me to believe. Papa grabbed up Mr. Sullivan by the collar and literally threw him out of the house, to the shock of both Mr. Hunter and me.

Mr. Sullivan looked appalled as he picked himself up. As he mounted his horse and waited for Mr. Hunter to mount, he shot another angry look at me. If eyes could kill, I would've been dead under his fiery gaze.

CHAPTER FOUR

Three weeks later, Travis Sullivan dropped by the house. He came by to apologize for his brother's rudeness and to say they'd caught the wolf that was killing the sheep.

"Funny, that wolf looked nothing like Chance," Travis said. "Anyway, I'm sorry on behalf of my brother."

Mama and Papa accepted the apology, but I still had my reservations about it. I did thank him for coming, and he did seem interested in Chance. He even walked up to her and kneeled down to pet her. Chance seemed to like him.

"She's beautiful. I'm glad Cal took her to you. Ethan would have killed her for sure."

"I know, and he still wants to kill her," I said.

He leaned down and looked into her eyes. "I can see why you want to keep her alive."

"Thank you. Look, I'm sorry if Cal got in trouble bringing her to me. I guess he really wanted Chance to be alive, too."

"Can't say I blame him. We all knew if we left her there, Ethan would kill her. I don't know, but it's like Ethan gets enjoyment from killing things sometimes. Now Cal, he's completely different. He has this thing about animals. He wants to save them all."

"He's a very sweet boy and doing well at school," I said, smiling. "I was just reading his essay. Would you like to read it?"

He blushed and looked down at Chance. "Truth is, ma'am, I ain't never learned to read that good. I know most of the good book. My mama read it to me, and I remembered most of the passages."

"But Travis, I remember we were in school together. I know your mama was so proud that her boys were able to read and write."

"Well, she taught us the good book, like I said. I know some of it, but that paper you have in your hand? I can't read it. Heck, Miss Annie, you know that when the war started out, we all were needed on the farm with Ethan and the others gone."

"Yes, I know, but if you like, I can teach you, Travis."

"Miss Annie, I'm too old to learn."

"That's not true. Why, I have a few people that I teach three days a week after dinner. They come to the school in private, and no one has to know. I would love to help you."

"I don't think so, but thank you for offering." He went outside, got up on his horse, and tipped his hat to me.

"If you ever change your mind, the offer is still there," I said.

He gave me one last smile and rode off. Somehow, I felt I had embarrassed him, though I truly hadn't meant to.

The next time I saw Travis Sullivan was at the church social. He was standing with his brother Abel. They were the only unmarried Sullivan boys in the family. Travis did look a bit out of place. Dressing up was not something he seemed to enjoy even though he looked handsome in his proper clothes.

I gave him a polite smile, and he returned it. Mayor Fitzgerald walked up to me and asked me to dance. Being polite, I took his hand and walked to the dance floor with him. I watched as Mama and Papa started to dance, too. Out of the corner of my eye, I noticed Travis looking my way.

I found Travis more handsome every time I looked at him, especially his intriguing green eyes. I couldn't help turning my head and looking at him directly. Yes, with his wheat-colored hair, strong jawline, and perfectly formed mouth, he was the most handsome man at the party.

Mama later told me she had seen me gaze toward Travis. Mama never was one to miss anything even when she was dancing across the room. How she was able to enjoy dancing with Papa and still keep an eye on her unmarried daughter was beyond me.

Throughout the night, I danced with quite a few gentlemen, but not once did Travis Sullivan come across the room and ask me for a dance, to my disappointment.

When the night was over, and everyone was leaving, Ethan Sullivan's wife, Sarah, came up to Mama and Papa.

"Mr. and Mrs. Lochlan, thank you for being so considerate about my husband's allegations. I heard from Mr. Henry what he said about Annie. He really had no right to say those things about your daughter. She's a lovely young woman. So many of the children are thrilled to have her as their teacher, including my Cal."

Mama smiled at her. "Mrs. Sullivan, there is no need. I'm just glad no one was hurt."

"No, just Ethan's pride, and that can heal. Sometimes pride can be a terrible thing, Mrs. Lochlan."

Sarah smiled as I walked toward her. "Miss Annie, my Cal speaks mighty highly of you, and I thank you for helping him with his learning. I thank you for giving him his dreams of being better than just a poor farmer. Before you came to teach, I never saw Cal look at a book. He's now reading and enjoying it."

"Well, Mrs. Sullivan, I can't take all the credit. Cal is a bright boy, and I feel he will go very far in school."

"For sure, Miss Annie? It would be a dream come true if all my youngins would know how to read and write—to do something more in life than me and his pa."

"I can promise you I will help him."

"Thank you, and God bless you."

She turned to leave. Her husband was waiting for her, standing at the door. His eyes met mine, and the look in them sent shivers down my spine.

I knew the man didn't want his family anywhere near town folk. He didn't want his son to have an education because he didn't have one. He knew enough to get by, and he could write his name, but that was it. In that respect, he was a lot like his father.

I'd met the late Mr. Sullivan only once in all the times I was in their home. I'd heard him yelling at Mrs. Sullivan. I had feared that if I hadn't been there, he would have hit her. Like Ethan, he claimed that as long as his sons knew how to farm, that was all the education they needed.

Agatha Sullivan had tried to teach the younger ones how to read and write. But with Ethan and the older ones, it was too late, and they had no interest in school anyhow.

My theory was that children imitated their parents. Since the Sullivan boys saw their father abusing their mother, they might have felt that behavior was acceptable. Perhaps some of them even thought that it was right. I watched Ethan grab his wife's arm and drag her out of the hall.

Our drive home was relatively quiet except for Mama and Papa teasing each other about their dancing. I just kept thinking of Sarah Sullivan and what Ethan would do to her.

"Now, Abby, I know I've caught you leading me more than once," Papa teased.

"Ryan, how could you say that? That's not true." She turned to me. "Annie, you're very quiet. That was a lovely compliment Mrs. Sullivan gave you. She is really excited about how well her son is doing in school."

"I wish I could get her to come to the adult classes."

"Oh, I doubt Ethan would let that happen. He's a stubborn man."

"He's a tyrant—that's what he is. It's like he's keeping them in the Middle Ages."

Papa gave me a stern look. "Annie, I have discussed with you a few times about your outbursts. I know you have an opinion on many things, but you have a way of saying them at the wrong time. Ethan Sullivan has his own way of dealing with his family, and in all these years, the Sullivans have kept to themselves. It's not going to change because you want them all to learn."

"But Papa, it's not just him. I offered to teach his brother Travis how to read, and he ran off like I was carrying the plague."

Papa did have to laugh at that one, and so did Mama, but I didn't see what was so funny. Before I could ask Papa, his face turned cold.

We were nearing the front of our house.

"Ryan, the door!" Mama cried.

The door was open.

"I see it," Pa said. He stopped the wagon a few yards from the house and got out. "Abby, you and Annie stay here. I'll check it out."

I handed him the rifle from the back of the wagon. "Here ya go, Papa."

"Thanks."

When Pa left, I suddenly realized Chance was in the house. I had left her upstairs in the bedroom.

"Where are you going?" Mama asked.

"To the back. What if she got out? If someone were in the house, she would be barking. I want to know if Chance is safe."

"But you know what your Pa said."

"I won't go inside the house. I don't hear Chance. She must be in the back. I'll go check and bring her back."

Before Mama could say another word, I got out of the wagon and crept toward the back of the house. When I got close, I collided with someone who was running out. The last thing I was conscious of was falling to the cold ground.

CHAPTER FIVE

The next day, I sat up in bed and found Doc Seaver beside me. He gave me a clean bill of health and told me I could go back to work on Monday. "I would like you to take it easy for the rest of the day, Annie. If you get dizzy or have headache, have someone get in touch with me. I want your promise you'll stay in bed."

"Okay, Doc."

Chance, as always, was by my side, which didn't bother the doc. He loved animals, and Chance liked him, too.

The doc had told me to stay in bed and rest, but I wanted to get up. Now, I knew there was nothing wrong with me going downstairs and maybe even getting some fresh air, but the trick was to do it without anyone catching me. Slowly, with Chance ahead of me, I snuck down the stairs, holding onto the rail.

I was in the hallway when I heard my mother's voice. "Annie, what are you doing out of bed? I know you heard Doctor Seaver tell you to stay in bed all day today. And you sat there and told him you would obey his orders."

"I'm really fine. I can't stay in that bed anymore, and Chance is here in case I get dizzy."

"And I suppose Chance will be able to tell us if you are in trouble?"

"Of course she will. She can bark."

Mama shook her head and pointed upstairs. "I suggest you march back upstairs and take your friend up there with you."

"Come on, Chance, let's go back up. Maybe we can tie my bed sheets together and climb out the window."

I was on my way up when the sound of horses coming up the road caught my attention. I looked out the window to see nearly the entire Sullivan clan approaching our home. Ethan, Abel, Thaddeus, Jonah, Eli, and Travis had all stopped at our front door.

"Mama, it's the Sullivan family."

Chance sat up, and her ears were pressed back.

"Easy, Chance. They're not gonna hurt anyone."

Ethan got off his horse first and knocked on the door. I opened the door and boldly met his gaze.

"Good afternoon, Miss. Is your pa home?"

"I suppose so, sir."

At that moment, Papa came to the door. "Something I can do for you, Ethan?"

"Heard your place was broke into last night. Heard your girl was hurt, knocked down as he was escaping."

"That's right."

"Our place was broke into also. No one was home."

"They get anything of value?" Papa asked.

"No. It seems we got there when he had just broken in," Ethan said.

"It seems they got nothing at my house, either. Something must have scared them off."

"The sheriff seems to think it's kids with too much time on their hands."

"Has anyone looked in on Henry Hunter and the missus?" Pa asked.

"I sent one of my men there this morning and told him meet us here."

"We can't do anything," Pa said, "and no one saw anything."

Ethan looked back at his brothers. "Come on. Let's go check on the Hunters."

They turned and rode out as fast as they'd ridden in. I met Travis's eyes for a second before he turned and followed them.

I thought about the look on Ethan's face and somehow knew he would track the intruder down the way he did with the animals he hunted.

CHAPTER SIX

Three weeks later, the sheriff solved the mystery of the intruders.

It turned out that Cal Sullivan and Johnny Crawford had wanted to see if they could break into a home and get out without a trace.

They'd tried to break into the Shirley house, but the dog had barked at them and alerted the gardener to their presence. The boys were taken to the sheriff's office, where they were placed in the custody of their fathers.

They confessed that they'd first broken into the Crawford home and the Sullivan home for practice and then gone inside the Lochlan home. Cal ran when he saw our wagon coming up the road, and Johnny followed. Johnny was the one who'd run into me.

That also solved the mystery of why Chance didn't bark or act up—she knew Cal.

Sam Crawford was a peaceful man who worked hard at keeping food on the table for his eight young ones. He was not in favor of what his son had done and thought it was wrong. He was grateful that I was not hurt more due to their prank, and he pulled Johnny out of school for two weeks, making him work on his farm instead.

Ethan was not as kind. Cal was not to attend school for the rest of the month. He was not allowed to leave the farm, and Ethan kept an eye on him all that time. Everyone thought they would never see Cal back at school or even in town again. Truth was, I felt the same way myself. I feared that Ethan would beat the boy. Everyone knew Ethan had had a mean streak since he'd come back from the war.

Days passed, and the boyhood prank was soon forgotten. In the fall, the townsfolk got ready for the first social of the season. It was a masquerade ball, and everyone was invited. Almost everyone attended in a costume.

Mama and Papa were Romeo and Juliet. Mr. and Mrs. Jenkins from the general store were old King Cole and his wife. Doc Seaver and his wife were Cinderella and Prince Charming. Many of the children chose to be the characters from their favorite bedtime stories, such as fairies, witches, and even ghosts.

I thought long and hard about my costume and ultimately settled on being a queen. Mama helped with my gown, which was a deep-green velvet material with gold brocade as an accent. The gown was heavy but lovely, and I felt beautiful in it.

In the October evening, the heavy velvet of my gown guarded me against the cold. Once we were all inside, we kept the church hall open to avoid the stuffiness of the hall. At first it was cold, but when everybody came, the place warmed up.

Children loved the games and, of course, the sweets. I noticed Cal Sullivan in the crowd, enjoying himself. He gave me a smile. I wondered if his father had lifted his punishment. That didn't sound like Ethan, and I hoped Cal was not there without his father's knowledge. I shuddered to think what Ethan would do in that case.

Doc Seaver was being a true Prince Charming by asking me to dance with him. I of course agreed, and we proceeded to walk to the dance floor and join the others there in a lovely waltz.

"How are you feeling, Annie? Or should I say, Your Majesty?"

"Just fine, Doc. Or is it Your Highness of Fall River? Is that the reason you asked to dance with me? And here I thought I had you under my spell."

"Of course not. I thought I'd get the first dance with the lovely Royal Highness Queen Annie Margarete since I know you'll be too busy later with all the young men here tonight. I seem to see quite a few men who have been captured by your charms. I was just wondering how you were feeling. You did have a nasty accident last week."

"Well, I am really impressed you know my whole name. I can tell you that I have not had any dizziness or headaches, but I do have one problem."

He looked at me for an explanation.

"I have a problem of always leading when I dance with a handsome man," I said. "Especially when he's as handsome as the one I'm dancing with right now."

"Well, I won't tell if you don't."

"You've got yourself a deal, Doc."

We continued to dance around the floor a few times. Everyone was having a grand time with all the music and laughter. Suddenly the music stopped.

I turned my attention to the door, and there stood Ethan. He was not a very tall man, but his presence in that doorway made him look like a mountain.

His gaze was directly on Cal, who looked as though he feared for his life. Ethan walked over to the boy, grabbed his arm, and began to twist it while shaking him.

"What do you think you're doing here, boy? Did I give you permission for you to leave the house? Who said you could come here? Did I not say you were grounded until I say you can go anywhere? Well, answer me, boy!"

We all saw that the boy was in pain as Ethan gripped him hard. I had to do something to get his attention.

"Mr. Sullivan, do come and join us."

"You just keep away from my family, Missy. We don't need the likes of you putting fool notions in their heads. They don't need any learning. All they need to know is how to farm. We're farmers, and that's all we need to be."

"Mr. Sullivan, I—"

"I told you, Missy, we don't need your book learning!"

"I was just going to tell you to let go of Cal's arm before he loses circulation in it."

He looked down at Cal and let go of the boy's arm. Cal dropped to the floor.

I rushed over to him. "Does your arm hurt too badly, Cal?"

"It's all right, Miss Annie. I've had worse."

Ethan glared at me. "You have to keep a youngin straight."

"I understand that, but you don't need to use force. After all, Mr. Sullivan, one can achieve much more with kindness than with force."

"With all due respect, ma'am, I don't tell you how to teach, so you don't tell me how to raise my youngin."

Just then, Sarah Sullivan and Travis came to the door. The frightened look on her face showed me she feared the worst. "Ethan, what are you doing?"

"Woman, you get back home! This is none of your business. You leave my boy to me."

"I will not leave." Sarah looked firm. Ethan seemed surprised. She had probably never defied him before.

Cal looked afraid. Maybe he feared his father would lash out on her in front of the whole town.

"I'm okay, Ma. You don't have to worry."

She gently put her hand on Cal's cheek. "No you're not. You're hurting, and he's not going to do this to you anymore."

Ethan raised his hand to hit his wife, but Papa grabbed it and knocked him down. "Sullivan, you'd better go home before I do something I might regret."

Ethan's face turned red. "You have no right, Lochlan. This is none of your business. This is my wife. She belongs to me, and she goes when I say."

"She's your wife, but she belongs to no one but herself. Your brother will take them home after Cal has his arm looked at."

"I won't forget this, Lochlan. You got a fine wife and daughter of your own there. Wouldn't want anything to happen to them."

Papa looked at him with a fire in his eyes I rarely saw. "Don't you dare come near my family, Sullivan, and if anything happens to them, you'll be the first one I'll hunt down."

Ethan got up and strutted toward the door. He turned around once to glare at everyone before leaving.

When he left, I walked over to the Sullivans. "Mrs. Sullivan, why don't you, Cal, and Travis come over to our table?"

Cal and his mother agreed and came over. Travis stayed by the door, making sure Ethan rode off.

"I couldn't let him hurt Cal anymore, Miss Annie," Sarah said. "He has such a fierce temper. I thought he'd tear his arm off."

"You don't have to stay with him," I said.

She looked like a frightened woman just then—not the strong woman who'd told Ethan off earlier but a frail wife who was used to being abused physically and mentally by her husband.

"You shouldn't worry. It's just that Ethan doesn't believe in all this education. He feels that we are plain folk and should live that way. I really do think I'd better get back home with Cal. Ethan will be waiting up for us to get back. You don't need to worry. Travis will take good care of us. After all, Ethan's my husband."

I looked up, and there was Travis, coming toward us. "I'll take good care of them, Miss Annie."

"I'm counting on you, Mr. Sullivan," I said, worried. I gave him a small smile, and he smiled back as he escorted his sister-in-law and Cal out the door. Pa came up behind me.

"You sure it was wise to send them back, Annie?"

"I couldn't keep them here. I'd be no better than her husband if I did that."

"You're right. I just worry."

"I know, Papa. So do I."

CHAPTER SEVEN

When I went to school to teach in the morning, I kept thinking about how Ethan had too much anger to just let it pass.

Papa and Ethan's wife had stood up to him in front of the town. I felt sure someone would have to pay for that. I didn't realize how true it would be.

Johnny Crawford told the class that he'd seen Travis and Cal carry Sarah Sullivan into Doc Seaver's office. She was in really bad condition. Johnny said Mrs. Sullivan was not moving at all.

I tried to keep my students' minds off Johnny's story, but I also wanted to go and see what happened. But I couldn't leave the class until it was over.

The school day dragged on, and it seemed that it would never end. I decided to let the class out a bit early for the day. It wouldn't take me long to go to the doctor's office and still be back to teach the evening class.

I rushed down the hill toward town and the doctor's office. When I got to the door, I ran into the sheriff, who was leaving.

"Afternoon, Miss Annie."

"Afternoon, Sheriff. Is Mrs. Sullivan all right?"

The sheriff let out a slow sigh. "I'm not going to lie to you. She's been hurt pretty bad. I think it would be better if you stayed out here for a bit."

"Is Cal all right? Does he need a place to stay while his mom–"

"The doc is having them stay at his place until Mrs. Sullivan regains consciousness. I don't think she should have any visitors right now."

"I see. Well, if I can't see them, I'll go back up the school and wait for my evening class."

He tipped his hat and headed to the other side of the street toward his office. I smiled and walked back up the hill to the school. As I sat waiting for the students to arrive, I was surprised to see Travis walk in the door.

"Miss Annie." He greeted me with a weak smile.

"Travis, hi. How is your sister-in-law?"

"Doc says she's banged up pretty bad—some broken ribs, her arm is broken, and her lip is split open." He started to break down. My heart broke for him. "He beat her so bad, Miss Annie. There was no reason for it. She only was singing a song when she was making supper. Poor Cal got his arm busted trying to stop him from hitting his ma. Ethan tossed the boy across the room like he was a rag doll. When I got there, I heard Cal screaming for him to stop hitting his ma. Ethan saw me come in the door and ran out the back door. I would have gone after him, but I wanted to get Sarah to the doctor since she looked pretty bad and lost a lot of blood."

"I'm so sorry. I feel that it's my fault for starting with him at the dance."

"No, it's been going on for years. Ethan has a bad temper. He's been a different man ever since he came back from the war."

The class started to come in, and Travis looked as though he wanted to leave.

"I'll stop by the doc's after I'm done with class. If you and Cal need a place to stay, you both can come out to the house."

"Thank you, Miss Annie. I'll leave you to your class now."

He tipped his hat and headed out the door, smiling politely at the ladies who were seating themselves at the desks.

I began to teach again. "Well, ladies, shall we pick up where we left off last week?"

After the evening class ended, I rushed to the doc's office once again.

"Well, hello, Annie," the doc said when he opened the door. "You're here rather late. Is there anything wrong?"

"No, I just came to see how Mrs. Sullivan was doing."

"She's still unconscious, and she's banged up pretty bad. Her son is with her, and his uncle is, too. I tried to get them to go get something to eat, but they won't leave. They say they're staying here till she wakes up."

"Maybe I can help, Doc."

"I was going to get some supper," he said. "The missus has made something for the boy and his uncle. I'll go get it. You're welcome to stay with them till I get back."

"Thank you."

I placed my books down on the end table and started up the stairs just as the sheriff was coming down. "Miss Annie, may I ask where you're going?"

"I was going to see how Mrs. Sullivan was doing."

"Well, I'm sorry, Miss Annie, but Mrs. Sullivan is still not in any condition to see visitors."

"When will she be ready?"

"When I get some answers," he replied.

"Answers?"

"I still have to speak to Ethan about what happened."

"You have to speak with Ethan? But look at Cal and Sarah. Good Lord, Sheriff—who could have possibly done this much damage but Ethan? You know how violent he can be. And you want to know what he was doing?"

"I'm not saying that it wasn't him. I'm saying by law I have to hear his side of this."

"Then why don't you ask him?" I said.

"I'm planning to as soon as I find him."

"You're telling me he's missing?"

"No one has seen him since he left the house after he did this to his wife. That woman was beaten so bad I think he really would have killed her this time if his brother hadn't rushed in to stop it."

I lowered my head. "I'm sorry. I had no right to come down on you."

He put his hand in my shoulder. "I understand, Miss Annie. Believe me—we are all a bit troubled by this. But, as I say, we have to hear both sides of the story, and we will once I find Ethan."

He helped me put my shawl back on and walked me out the door. I couldn't help wondering about Ethan, who was out there somewhere. What if he wasn't finished hurting people?

CHAPTER EIGHT

Luckily, Sarah Sullivan regained consciousness on the third day after arriving at the doc's. Despite all her injuries, the doc thought she would be able to move around very slowly in another week or two.

Cal's arm was broken in two places but was healing nicely. But then again, a nine-year-old was able to bounce back quicker than an adult. He'd be using both arms again in no time.

Two weeks passed, and we still found no sign of Ethan. With Thanksgiving only a week away, Mama was getting the house ready for the family to arrive.

Uncle Mick and Aunt Mary were coming, and so were my sisters, Meghan and Molly, and my brothers, Tom and Daniel, as well as all their spouses and children.

Uncle Mick and Aunt Mary and their two children were the first due to arrive. Uncle Mick was so much fun. He always made us laugh, and he and Papa were the best of friends.

Papa and I sat in the carriage as we waited for their train. When it pulled into the station, I saw Aunt Mary waving from the window.

She came out of the train and gave me a big hug. Aunt Mary had been just a young girl when we were born. With only fifteen years between us, she was more like a sister than an aunt.

The reunion of Uncle Mick and Papa was short-lived because the sheriff came over and pulled Papa aside to speak to him. The two spoke for a while. I had no idea what was going on, but when Papa walked back to us, the expression on his face told me that it was not good.

"Annie, I need to go with the sheriff. Uncle Mick will get you all home. I will be home as soon as I can."

"But Papa, it's Thanksgiving."

"I know, sweetheart. Don't worry. I'll be home before you know it."

Uncle Mick interjected. "Look, Ryan, Annie can drive Mary and the children. I'm coming with you."

"Mick, it's not—"

"The discussion is over, Sir Galahad. I'm going with you."

I did what I was told and drove my aunt and cousins back to the farmhouse, where a very impatient Mama was waiting.

"Where is your father?" she asked.

"He and Uncle Mick had to go somewhere with the sheriff."

"Oh, I'll wring his bloody neck! I told him to come back, and no short stops. Why of all people did I marry a stubborn Irishman?"

Aunt Mary looked at her sister, smiling and shaking her head. "You know they are never going to change, Abby. Both of them, it's like they are playing hooky. They're like little boys who never really grew up. But I will say the sheriff did come up and ask Ryan to speak with him."

"Oh, Mary, don't you fall for his tricks, too. That man knew I wanted him to help with the upstairs bedroom, and he took off. He probably had the sheriff in on it, and you know Mick—he's always ready to go somewhere."

"Well, we're here, and I'm sure Peyton would help." Mary looked at her son. "Wouldn't you, Peyton?"

Peyton had grown so much since we'd last seen him. Soon, he'd be going off to college.

"Of course," Peyton said.

The following morning, the sheriff knocked on the door of my family's farm. I was the one who answered the door.

"Good morning, Miss Annie. Is your pa around?"

"Yes. If you'd like to come in, I'll get him for you."

"Why, yes, thank you." He stepped inside and followed me to the dining room.

"The sheriff's here," I announced.

Pa and Uncle Mick looked up. Uncle Mick was the first to comment. "Well, I'm sorry, Sheriff, but I won't go peacefully until after I've had my breakfast. By the way, you should have some also." He smiled and started to attack the bacon and eggs on his plate.

Mama walked up to the sheriff. "Can I get you some coffee, Tom? How about some breakfast?"

"Why, coffee would be mighty nice, Mrs. Lochlan."

Mama put down the coffee pot and looked at him. "Tom, how long have we known each other?"

"'Bout fifteen years now, ma'am."

"Well, I think it's time you called me Abby. Matter of fact, I demand that you call me Abby."

Papa looked over the rim of his coffee cup. "Take it from me, Tom—when my wife demands something, she usually gets it. She has this way of haunting you until you agree."

With that comment, everyone at the table began to chuckle.

"Tell me, Sheriff, have you found Ethan Sullivan yet?" I asked.

"No, we haven't."

"Well then, what are you doing here?"

"Annie!" Ma exclaimed. "You apologize to Tom right this instant."

I got up and went upstairs. I heard Mama trying to smooth things over. "I'm sorry, Tom. I don't know what got into her."

At the top of the stairs, I didn't go into my room. Instead, I stopped and listened.

"Oh, I know. Heck, we're all upset about this. That's why I'm here. I wondered if Ryan or Mick had come across any old mine shafts or caves a person could hang out in for a while."

Mama looked at Papa and Mick.

"I'm not sure," Papa said, "but I think I have some old maps we had when we worked for the railroad. There might be some locations on them."

"That would a big help. Seems there's a feeling that he may be hiding out, waiting for all this to blow over."

"What about his brothers? Haven't any of them seen him?"

"Well, Abel and the others were up on the north range. They want to get the herd of sheep down before the snow falls and they lose most of them. Travis was at the Hunter farm. He's been helping the old man. Ole Henry is not as spry as he once was, and Travis has been helping him with his crops. I had to check his story, and the Hunters stated he was at their place and has been there everyday, except that he has been in town at the doc's with Cal since Tuesday. I got his story about how he saw Ethan leaving but decided to take Sarah to the doc's."

"Thank goodness he did. She may not have made it if he hadn't. She was pretty bad when he got her to there."

Papa came back into the dining room with three scrolls in his hands.

"I have some maps here that may help. I figure if we divide the men into three groups, each one taking a map, we can cover more ground. Now, the main thing you have to remember is that not all these caves are deep. I would concentrate on the lower ones since those higher up could have company in them this time of year. Wolves like high places out of the wind."

"Seems like a good idea," the sheriff said. "We'll keep to the lower sections."

Papa moved the dishes off the table and spread out one of the maps.

"As you can see, these are basically where the tracks would be easier to follow. Also, it shows a number places that would be excellent for a person or persons to hide out should they care to."

The sheriff looked at the map and agreed that it was a lot of land to cover but worth a try.

"Okay. I would like to get started on this as soon as possible. Mick, Ryan—I'd like you two to take a map each, and I'll take the last one. The first one to find anything, send someone to alert the others to join you."

They both agreed, and the sheriff took a last sip of his coffee and headed for the door. "I'll tell the others, and we'll all meet in town in about an hour."

With the snow starting to fall, along with the temperature, we all wondered how long Ethan would be able to stand being out there and whether they'd be able to bring him back alive.

I left for town earlier the next morning. Before I got to the school, I thought I'd stop at Doc Seaver's. I got off the wagon and looked around, making sure no one saw me. I gently tapped on the door. Doc Seaver opened the door and smiled at me.

"Annie Lochlan, what can I do for you?"

"I was wondering how Mrs. Sullivan was doing."

"Oh, she's getting along just fine. Is there anything else I can do for you?"

I knew he as not going to let me in.

"No thanks, Doc. Just was wondering how she was. And Cal—is he also okay?"

"Cal is coming along fine. His uncle will bring him to school tomorrow before he leaves for Mr. Hunter's farm."

"Well, I'd better get going. Thanks, Doc."

I was turning to leave when I saw Travis Sullivan drive up with the wagon. He smiled and tipped his hat to me. "Miss Annie."

I smiled back, genuinely happy to see him. "Mr. Sullivan."

He stopped the wagon near the doc's and got off. He took his hat off when he walked up to me. "I left Cal at school. I know Doc said he could go tomorrow, but he wanted to go today. I hope it's okay."

"I was just asking Doc about him. I should get up to the school—I don't want him standing out there."

"I'll pick him up after school today if that's all right."

"Of course," I said. "I'll make sure he's ready when you come by."

"Thanks, Miss Annie."

"You're welcome, Mr. Sullivan."

I was about to leave when I heard his voice again. "My name is Travis, ma'am."

I turned and smiled at him. "You're welcome, Travis."

The smile on his face was priceless.

"Oh, do tell Mrs. Sullivan I was asking after her," I said.

"Will do."

After a lingering gaze on me, which made me blush, he knocked on the door, and the doc let him in. He turned around and smiled at me again before he closed the door.

I got back into the wagon and headed up the hill to the schoolhouse. There, Cal sat waiting for me on the front steps. I rode up and got off the wagon to greet him.

"I was just at Doc's, asking about you and your ma," I told him cheerfully.

"She's coming along fine, Miss Annie. Hope we can take her back home soon."

"That would be wonderful. Well, I guess we should get school started."

For the past three days, the sheriff, Papa, and other ranchers had been looking for Ethan but with no luck. By that time, the brothers had joined in on the search.

Sarah Sullivan was recovering from her husband's beatings but still had far to go. Once the bruises and scars faded away, the inner scars and nightmares would take longer to heal—if they ever did. Mama offered to let her, Cal, and Travis stay at our house until Sarah was well enough to go back to her home. Mama was like that. If anyone needed help, she was always there.

At the end of the week, that I noticed the Sullivan's wagon in front of our house. I drove up slowly before stopping.

Cal came out the door and waved. "Miss Annie, we're gonna spend some time here at your place."

"Why, that's fine, Cal. Just fine."

As I turned, I saw Travis standing at the door, looking as dashing as ever. "Sarah would like to speak with you, Miss Lochlan."

"Then I should go right in. Thank you, Travis. Oh, by the way, my name is Annie."

"Yes, ma'am."

He held the door open for me, and as I walked into the hall, Mama appeared.

"Hi, Mama. I was just going to see Sarah."

"She's in Grandpa's old room."

I set my books down and headed to the room. I tapped on the door lightly.

"Come in," a weak voice answered.

I opened the door and saw for the first time what Ethan had done to her. Sarah's face was still badly bruised. Both of her eyes were swollen. Her arm was in a cast, and her lip was cut and swollen. I felt so sorry for the poor woman, but I tried not to show it.

"Mrs. Sullivan, Travis said you wanted to speak to me?"

It was hard for her to articulate her words because of her cut lip, but I did understand what she was trying to say.

"I would like you to teach me how to read and write. Could you do that, Miss Annie?"

"I would be happy to, Mrs. Sullivan."

A tear escaped her eye as she tried to smile.

"Can I get you anything? Some water, or another pillow?

"Take care of my Cal until I can get around again. I don't want him to worry about me. I don't want his father to get him."

"Mrs. Sullivan, no one has seen him since the accident."

She closed her eyes and smiled. "Maybe he's gone for good this time. Oh, dear Lord, forgive me for saying such a thing." She turned to look at me. "Miss Annie, my son gave you that pup because he felt you would be kind to her and see that she was just a baby. I see now he was right—you truly are a gentle soul. I'm asking you not to judge Ethan for this. It's just that something comes over him, and he can't help it."

"I'm not here to judge him, Mrs. Sullivan..."

"I know it's wrong, but when you find someone you love, you'll understand."

I didn't want to upset her, but I didn't ever want to feel that I would love someone so much I would let them do that to me. I saw she was drifting off to sleep again, so I quietly backed out of the room.

As I closed the door, I saw that Cal had come up the stairs and was behind me. "How is Ma, Miss Annie?"

"Oh, she's coming along. She's still a bit tired and is resting now."

"That's okay. I'll just go in and sit there until she wakes up."

I smiled as he slowly opened the door and walked in. I went out to the hall and saw Chance. I leaned down and patted her head and made my way out front door with her by my side. As we stepped outside, Travis rose to his feet.

"It's all right," I told him. "She won't hurt you."

"Oh no, Miss Annie—I wasn't afraid of her. Heck, I knew when Ethan took her home that day he wanted to kill her right off. That was when Cal said he wanted to bring her as a gift for the new teacher, and I convinced Ethan to let him do it. Cal figured other kids would bring you normal gifts like candy, handkerchiefs, flowers, and such. He wanted to give you something special."

I looked at Chance and nodded. "Well, she sure is special." I looked up and saw him smiling. "You have a very nice smile, Travis. You should smile more often."

"I will, Miss Annie, when I find a reason to smile."

"Then I hope you find many reasons to smile."

CHAPTER NINE

Every day after school, I helped Mrs. Sullivan with her lessons. She knew her Bible very well, although she'd memorized a lot of it. Her goal was to be able to write, and with my help, she reached that goal in the third week.

Mrs. Sullivan also slowly began to get around. She offered to help Mama in the kitchen, but Mama said she just enjoyed her company. Having someone to talk to was refreshing. It got lonely around the empty house during the day. Besides, Mama told her, she was a guest, and guests didn't work in the Lochlan house, but Mrs. Sullivan was welcome to help make the shopping list since Thanksgiving was only two weeks away. The two women decided to combine their recipes to give both families a great family holiday feast.

Ethan was still out there somewhere. Sometimes, Mrs. Sullivan worried that he was still alive. The weather was getting colder by the day. One day, Travis came with news: Abel Sullivan had noticed footprints outside the barn when he'd gone to milk the cows in the morning.

Both Abel and his brother Jonas realized that the prints were Ethan's because of the boot size. Since the footprints were leading away from the barn, they knew that Ethan couldn't be there anymore. But they also knew that Ethan was still alive and had spent the night there in the barn. Perhaps he'd been scared off by the search party, but where did he go after that?

The brothers agreed that if Ethan had been hiding out in the caves in the hills, he'd be like a wild animal, ready to lash out at anything. And if he was in one of his moods, they'd never be able to get him to come back. Still, they had to tell the sheriff.

In the early afternoon, the sheriff rode up to our home. I was on the porch with Travis as the sheriff dismounted and smiled at us.

"Miss Annie, Mr. Sullivan."

"Good morning, Sheriff. Is there anything I can help you with?"

"Well, yes. I'm looking for your father."

"He just went into town with Mama," I said. "My sisters are coming for the holiday. They should be home in a bit. The train was due in at 1:05."

The sheriff looked at his pocket watch. "It's 1:30 now. If the train was on time, they should be on their way back."

"Like I said, Sheriff, you are welcome to stay."

"Thank you. I think I will."

Before long, they rode up in the wagon. Along with my parents, Molly had come with her husband, Braxton, as well as Meghan and her husband, Adam, and their little ones. Aunt Mary and Uncle Mick were already inside our house.

Papa brought the carriage to a stop. Braxton was the first one out so that he could help the ladies down.

Papa approached the sheriff.

The sheriff greeted him. "Is there a place we can talk privately?"

"In my study."

"Good."

Papa passed Uncle Mick, who had just walked out the door with Aunt Mary to greet the girls along with Travis and me. "Mick, would you handle the—"

The sheriff interrupted. "If you don't mind, I'd like Mr. Dawson in on this also."

At that point, Travis got up and walked over to the bags. There were plenty of men to help the ladies, so Mick, the sheriff, and Papa walked through the hall and straight to the back where the library was.

Chance was so excited she was jumping on everyone. I had a hard time telling her to sit. Molly beamed when she saw the pup, but she gave me a weird look.

"Annie, dear, do you know that—"

"Yes, she's a wolf. Not to worry. She doesn't know she's one."

Braxton was impressed. "How did you get her?"

"One of my students thought it was a nice gift for the new teacher."

Adam took one look at the pup and shielded the children.

"Honestly, Adam," I said. "Chance won't hurt the children."

As everyone settled in, Molly told me about the conversation she'd had with the family on the wagon ride home. It had started when she asked Mama, "How did you do it, having three babies all at once?"

Mama smiled. "Well, at times I wondered how I would get through, but I was very lucky—I had your Aunt Mary, Jenny, Uncle Mick, your father, and Grandpa Daniel."

They turned onto the road that would lead them right to the house, and Meghan recognized the sheriff. "Ryan, is that Tom on the porch with Annie and Travis?"

"Travis?" Molly asked.

"You know Travis," Meghan said. "Travis Sullivan. His family has a farm north of us."

"They've been there for years," Mama added, "but they keep to themselves. When Annie was little, she used to go every Wednesday to the Sullivan home to have her piano lesson with Mrs. Sullivan."

Molly took a closer look at Travis as the wagon drew closer. "He is rather handsome. Is Annie interested in him?"

Mama smiled. "I think so. I just wish Annie knew it."

"Oh, Mama, I'm sure she knows," Meghan said. "Maybe he hasn't noticed her."

"Oh no—he definitely has noticed her. I think he's too shy to approach her."

The two sisters had looked at each other and smiled. Mama and Papa had also given each other a knowing look.

CHAPTER TEN

In the study, the sheriff was telling Papa why he was there.

"We got a tip from Abel Sullivan. He found some footprints outside the barn this morning, and they believe they're Ethan's. Now, they tell me that all along that north ridge, close by, are caves that people have used in the winter months to shield themselves from the snow."

"If you think he's hiding there, why don't you go and get him?" Papa asked.

"Because there are over twenty caves up there, and we have no idea which one he's in. Do you still have those maps we used before?"

Papa said, "Mick, could you go get the maps for the sheriff?"

Mick opened the door and ran into Mama, who was bringing in coffee for the gentlemen.

"A cup of coffee?" she asked.

"Thank you, Abby," the sheriff said.

"Abby, dear," Papa said, "I would like you to keep everyone away from this door."

"But why? What's wrong?"

"We have information that Ethan is held up in one of the many caves in the area. I don't want Travis or Sarah to get upset about it."

"All right. We'll keep them busy."

Mick came back in with the maps, and with the doors closed, the three men planned the best way to capture Ethan and to bring him off the mountain.

"Well, then, it's all set," the sheriff said. "Ryan, you take the little brother. Mick, you take Abel, and I'll take Jonas. We split up and check every cave. When you find him, give three shots then another three, and we'll come to you."

Papa looked at the sheriff in surprise. "In all fairness, we should first let Mrs. Sullivan know that her husband is alive—well, alive for the time being."

"For the time being?"

"Abel tells me there's no way of knowing what state of mind he's in right now, and if he thinks his wife is truly dead and we're looking so we can have him hanged, he might not come peaceably."

"All right. You tell her he's alive but nothing more."

They left the room, and Ryan headed to the door across the hall. He knocked and heard Sarah's voice inviting him in.

"Hi, Sarah."

"Hello, Ryan. How are you? I hope we're not taking up too much room with your family coming. We can always go back home.

"No, of course you don't need to. I just wanted to tell you that there is a good chance that Ethan is still alive. Abel found footprints near the outside of the barn this morning, and it's possible that Ethan spent last night there. There is a chance that he is holed up in one of the caves on the property. We've got three search parties going up and checking the caves to find him and bring him home."

She closed her eyes as tears rolled down her cheeks, but then she quickly looked at him with a worried expression. "You know he's not going to come home. He thinks I'm dead, and he thinks you are all going there to bring him back to hang him. You have to let him know that I'm alive!"

"Travis is coming with me, and Abel and Jonas are with the other search parties."

"I'm going with you. He will come back if he sees me alive."

"Sarah, you are in no condition to go anywhere," Pa said. "I promise to bring him back."

"I have to go!" she shouted, alerting Mama, who rushed in the room.

"What's wrong, Ryan?" Mama asked with great concern.

"She wants to go with the posse."

Mama sat Sarah down and tried to calm her.

"Don't be silly, dear. You're in no shape to climb anything. Now, just sit there."

"He won't believe Abel. He's going to think it's a trick. He doesn't need much to bring on one of his rages and... oh, Abby, they'll kill him! I have to go. Don't you understand?"

Sarah never calmed down completely, but she agreed to stay home with us while the men did their search. Within the hour, Papa and Travis were on their way to the mysterious caves. I had uneasy feeling about this and felt as if something bad was going to happen.

CHAPTER ELEVEN

Travis led Papa the back way to one of the caves he'd found years ago. It went through the mountain and came out through the other side. He said he was sure Ethan didn't know about it.

Slowly, they made their way through the massive tunnel that would lead them to Ethan. After what seemed like hours, they reached a last turn and saw the glow of firelight against the wall. Pa realized they were about to come upon Ethan.

As they approached, Ethan turned and aimed his gun at them.

Travis yelled out. "Ethan! It's me, Travis. Put the gun down! Ethan, we've come to take you back to town."

"I can't go back. Sarah's dead. I killed her."

"No, Ethan. She's not dead. She's been staying at the Lochlan farm until she got better."

Ethan looked at Travis. "My Sarah's alive? She's not dead?"

"Yes," Travis replied. "She's alive, and she's waiting for you at the Lochlan farm. I promised her I'd take you back home."

A smile came to his face. But it was quickly erased when the sheriff called out in front of the cave. "Ethan Sullivan, come out with your hands up. Give yourself up. You're surrounded."

Ethan looked at Travis and Ryan with wide eyes. "I thought you said Sarah was alive, Travis."

"She is, but the sheriff still has to take you in."

He stepped back into the cave. "I'm not going to jail. I will not go to jail. You, my own brother, lied to me. You want to see me hang!"

Ethan rushed to the side exit of the cave and aimed his gun at the opening to shoot anyone who would come up. Papa knew he had to do something to stop him from really killing someone, so he leaped and landed on Ethan, causing both men to tumble down a short incline to the outside of the cave. Papa had to get that gun from him. Ethan had the gun against Papa's throat, and it looked as though Ethan would kill him.

The sheriff was speeding his way up toward them when the gun went off.

Ethan stood up and walked back inside the cave. When he came into Travis's view, he staggered and fell face down.

Papa followed, looking as if the wind had been knocked out of him. Travis kneeled over his brother.

Papa seemed to have difficulty speaking. Finally, he said, "I'm sorry, Travis."

"I understand, Mr. Lochlan," Travis said. "You tried to take the gun away from him. If you hadn't tried, he would have shot us or the sheriff. He didn't believe us. He heard the sheriff and thought we were trying to trick him. He wasn't the Ethan we knew. It's what he turned into when the mood came over him. It finally killed him, and now he's at peace."

"I know, I know, but I still did it, and I feel as if I failed Sarah."

It took a while for the sheriff to reach the cave, followed by Mick and his group. Mick looked down at the body and then up at Ryan. "You didn't have a choice. It was him or you."

"I know," Papa said. "I just wished I'd had a little more time. Maybe I—"

Mick stopped him. "But you didn't, and you're lucky he didn't kill both of you. You took a chance walking into his hideout. You know that."

The men carried Ethan's body down from the cave, back to their horses.

"How am I going to tell Sarah that I killed her husband?"

"Mr. Lochlan" Travis said, "don't go worrying over this. If you like, I'll tell her."

Papa smiled. "I'll do it. I promised I would bring him home to her—I just didn't think it would be this way—but thank you."

CHAPTER TWELVE

Helped by Mama and Aunt Mary, Sarah Sullivan got into the wagon with Cal and me, and we drove into town to meet the posse. Abel was taking the horse with Ethan's body on it to the undertaker. The sheriff stopped when he saw Mrs. Sullivan.

"Mrs. Sullivan, I'm sorry that it had to end this way."

"I understand," Mrs. Sullivan said solemnly. "I knew he wasn't going to come back alive. That's why I begged to go. If he'd seen me, he would still be alive."

With Cal's help, she got down from the wagon and walked over to Abel and the horse. Slowly, she lifted the blanket that covered

Ethan's dead body. After a glimpse, she quickly lowered it again. "We'll make the arrangements now," she said to Abel.

Abel got off his horse and helped his sister-in-law into the undertaker's.

"We came when we got the news," Mama told Papa when he and Uncle Mick rode in. "Sarah wanted to be here when they took Ethan in. How did it happen?"

"He went for his gun, and I jumped on him to stop him from shooting the sheriff."

Uncle Mick just nodded, and they knew he needed to be left alone. It looked as if Papa was going through a battle in his own mind by this killing. He and Uncle Mick headed for the sheriff's office.

As Mama and Aunt Mary were waiting for Papa and Uncle Mick, Mrs. Sullivan came out and slowly walked over. With a lifeless expression, she said to Mama, "If you don't mind, I would like to go back to my home now. I will not be going back to your farm again."

"Sarah, you have just had a terrible shock. Don't you feel it's not the time to–"

"I thank you for your concern, Mrs. Lochlan, but I cannot and will not stay in the home of the man who killed my husband. He promised me he would bring him home to me. I didn't think it would be as a dead man."

Mama was shocked at her words, yet she understood why Sarah would feel that way. "I can let you borrow the wagon to get you back comfortably."

"That will not be necessary, Mrs. Lochlan. I will have Cal get me a carriage so I can drive to the house. I do thank you for your kindness."

"Mrs. Sullivan, do you really feel you have to leave? You could stay in town..."

She turned and looked at her. "I belong at home, Mrs. Lochlan. If I had gone with the posse, Ethan would still be alive today, but I listened to your husband. Now you have your husband, but mine is gone."

No one saw much of the Sullivans after that. Cal no longer went to school, and Travis stayed on the farm. Life did go on, and soon Fall River forgot all about Ethan Sullivan.

I continued to teach and still had my adult classes in the afternoon, but never again would Sarah Sullivan come to class or call on me. I felt bad for Cal. He was such a bright boy and so eager to learn.

The winter was hard and brutal. Many of the ranches around us lost stock, but once the snow melted, and the first signs of spring began to show, the warm weather soon followed. Everyone welcomed it.

On one of these lovely afternoons, Papa came home early that afternoon to find Mama in the living room, knitting. There was something in the air—a sense of rebirth, a new beginning.

He always said he never tired of seeing Mama smile and loved her more and more every day. As he walked to her that day, he fell and couldn't get back up. Papa smiled at Mama to maintain a brave face. "This is a bit silly," he said in a weak voice. "I felt a snap in my back, and now I can't move my legs."

Mama bolted out of her chair. "Annie will be home soon. She'll help lift you."

"Abby, I think you'd better turn on the light. It's getting dark out there."

"Hush, Ryan. It's better if you rest."

He smiled up at her. "I can't move my legs. My legs... I'm crippled."

"Ryan! Ryan, what's wrong?"

"Abby, you'll have to follow this dream alone. But don't worry, darlin'—I'll be waiting for you on the other side. I'll never leave you, ever. I love you, my sweet Abby."

With that, he passed from one world into the next with Ma holding his lifeless body.

CHAPTER THIRTEEN

My brother Daniel had gone into town to fetch the doc. When they came back, Travis was behind them on his horse. He'd run into Daniel at the doc's office and decided to hurry back with them.

Travis sat with me as I waited for the doc. When he came out of Pa's room, I stood up.

"I'm sorry, Annie. He passed away," the doc confirmed.

I stood there, holding Travis's hand as tight as I could. There were no tears. I didn't really believe he was gone. Not my papa. He'd been just fine that morning.

"What happened to him?" I asked.

"To tell you the truth, I can't figure it out. I can only guess he was poisoned somehow. It's the only thing that would spread through the system so fast."

I looked at the doc. "Poisoned? Who would poison Papa?"

The bedroom door opened, and slowly, Mama came out. Her face betrayed no emotion, but all the color was drained from her complexion. She had no tears, but I'd heard her crying behind the door while I waited.

I wanted to run to her, but Travis, who was still holding my hand, held me back. I turned to look at him, but he just shook his head. Mama walked up to the three of us. She had gathered all the composure she had in order to say her next words.

"Your father has passed. I need one of you to go into town to send wires to your sisters and Aunt Mary. Also, get Mr. Loring to come out. I want him to come out today. I'll make the arrangements when your sisters and Aunt get here."

She looked at Travis. "Mr. Sullivan, I thank you for your kindness and help. Ryan thought a lot of you. I'm sure you being here today eased his mind as he went on his new journey."

"Ma'am, if you don't mind," Travis said, "if there is anything I can do for you and Miss Annie, don't hesitate to ask."

"You are most kind." She thought for a moment. "Oh my, where are my manners? Can I offer you something? Annie, go get something for Mr. Sullivan. He's been sitting here all day. He must be thirsty."

Travis stopped her. "Ma'am, I'm fine. Can we get you anything?"

Mama looked at him, and then she simply went back into the room.

"I can give her a sedative," the doc said. "That should keep her calm."

"That would be fine, Doc."

I went inside to sit beside Ma, who was still staring at Pa's lifeless body. "I want you to take a pill the doc is going to give you. It will make you feel better."

Mama looked at me and then at the doctor, who was standing at the door. "I don't need anything, Doctor. I am perfectly calm."

"Right now, you are giving the impression that all is well, but you will crash. Please take the pill, Abby."

He handed the small pill to her. Reluctantly, Mama took it and put it in her mouth.

The doc watched her. "Abby, swallow the pill."

She swallowed the pill and turned to me. "Don't you have something to do?"

"If you want, I can go help Daniel in town." I looked out the window and saw that Pa's horse was still saddled.

"Okay."

"I'll be back as soon as I can, Mama."

As I headed out, Ma spoke to Travis. "Mr. Sullivan, would you be so kind as to escort my daughter into town?"

"Yes, ma'am."

He had his horse and would follow me. Before we left, I could hear Mama speaking to the doc. "That young man is going to marry my Annie. I can feel it in my bones."

CHAPTER FOURTEEN

Travis was almost wearing his horse out trying to catch up to me. He finally did and grabbed my horse's reins to slow him down. "Annie, you're gonna wear the horse out riding like that,"

"I have to get to my brother. And I'll thank you to get your hands off my reins."

"That's all well and good, but you have to take it easy on the horse."

I knew he was right, but I just had to keep going. "Mr. Sullivan, Snake Eyes is an excellent horse. He knows how much he can take. Look at his eyes. Don't they look like snake eyes?"

"Annie, enough! You're father has just passed, and you're—"

"I'm what? Look, I appreciate your concern, but I don't need your help."

"Well, need it or not, I'm staying with you! Right now you need someone. I've always wanted to be there for you, and you never noticed. You still don't, but I'm staying, so you might as well get use to it."

He let go of the reins. "Now, let's get moving. You have to get to town."

After the wires were sent to my sisters and Aunt Mary, we went to Mr. Loring's. Morton Loring was the town undertaker who had known my family for some time. He had handled the arrangements for my uncle Gideon and Grandpa Daniel and now Papa.

I didn't say a word to Travis on the way back home. I just kept hearing the words *I always wanted to be there for you.* He was my Galahad, and I'd never known it. All those years, he had been there, waiting for me to notice him. Of course, I'd liked him, but I never thought he cared for me that way.

Later that afternoon, Daniel moved Papa's body from the house, and Mama busied herself with getting the house ready for the family to arrive. I would find myself looking at the front door, hoping that Papa would walk through it, and that all this was only a bad dream. But it was not a dream, and Papa was gone.

I walked out to the rose garden, where I found Mama sitting, talking with Travis. She was telling him the story of how she and Papa met. I'd heard the story many times and never tired of it.

I went over to them and sat down as she came to the part I loved the best: the first time she opened that door and Papa was standing there.

As she was telling the story, Travis glanced over to me and smiled. I realized he was taking Mama's mind off what was really happening and giving her happier thoughts. It was his was his way of helping her cope with her grief.

Molly, Brax, and their children were the first to arrive on the noon train. They hired a carriage from the livery and rode out to the ranch. It was a bittersweet reunion as I opened the door. There were no tears. We had done that all already. It was time to stand by Mama.

Molly took the children in to see Mama while Brax and Travis took care of the luggage. Once the children had done their job to keep Grandma busy, Molly was able to speak to me. "What happened to Papa?"

"The doc seems to think poison somehow got into his system. We're still not sure how."

Shock came over Molly's face. "Who would want to do this to our father? Pa was so well loved by everyone."

At supper time, Meghan, Adam, and their children arrived, and the house became more like a family reunion than a family in mourning, which was what Papa would have wanted.

After the family arrived, the sheriff came to our door.

"Hi, Sheriff," I said. "Is there something I can do for you?"

"Annie, I'd like to speak to you and your sisters and your brothers if I may."

I didn't like the tone of his voice. "Is there something wrong?"

"I'd prefer to have all of you present when I tell you this."

"Please, come in. I'll get my siblings."

I gathered Molly, Meghan, Daniel, and Tom, and we all headed to the study. I passed by Travis on the way, and he looked at me curiously.

Once inside the office, the sheriff explained to us how the poison had entered our father's system. He explained that Sarah Sullivan had devised a plan with Cal. I was so shocked to hear this that I felt numb.

According to the confession that Cal had written, which was found by his body, his mother had told him it was his duty to kill Ryan because he'd shot Ethan.

Young Cal decided he couldn't take anymore and finally went along with her plan. He rode up to the north ridge, where he knew Papa was herding cattle, and offered him some of his lunch.

"I tell you, this is excellent fried chicken. Have yourself another piece, Mr. Lochlan. I brought enough for both of us."

Cal had poisoned the chicken that they both ate.

"I'm sorry," the sheriff told us. "Your pa didn't know what was happening, nor could he have stopped it before it was too late."

I looked at him. "But why Cal, Sheriff? He was such a sweet boy."

"His mother couldn't stop pressuring him. She never forgave your pa for Ethan's death."

"But Ethan was cruel to her and beat her so badly. You saw her the last time. And everyone said that Papa was trying to save the posse. They fought with the rifle between them. It went off, and no one could know who pulled the trigger. Ethan could have pulled it himself by mistake."

"Well, she went a little crazy in the head. For the past year, Sarah had time to torment the boy so badly she finally won. Maybe he went crazy, too. After Cal had lunch with Ryan, he decided to go back to the ranch write this confession and wait for the poison to take effect. He knew what he had done, and this may have been his point of remorse.

"Seems his mother turned him against all of you, but he did feel remorse. His mother must have come home and found him dead. The ranch hands heard a shot and rushed in and saw Cal in the chair, dead, and Sarah with the note in her left hand and a colt in her right. She had a bullet wound in her head. I can safely assume she realized she was responsible for Cal's death."

I couldn't believe my ears. Sarah Sullivan had pushed her son to the point where he'd felt he had to kill my papa.

I stormed out of the study and out the back door. There in the rose garden was Travis, sitting with Brax and Adam. Brax took one look at my face and moved out of my path.

I walked up to Travis and spoke directly to him. "I think you'd better leave. Seems your nephew and sister-in-law are dead."

He looked up with a startled expression. "How?"

"Cal poisoned my papa and then himself. Your sister-in-law kept blaming Papa for Ethan's death."

He tried to talk, but I turned and left.

CHAPTER FIFTEEN

The service lasted longer than expected because so many of the townspeople wanted to pay their respects before the mass. The church was packed with people who wanted to say their last words to Papa. The procession of friends followed the coach ride back to the house.

We had decided that Papa would be placed to rest near those he loved and who loved him: Daniel, Molly, Gideon, Jenny, and Annie, Ma's little sister who I was named after.

When all were at the gravesite, Uncle Mick stepped up to deliver the eulogy we'd asked him to do for the man who was more a brother to him than a friend. We all had tears rolling down our faces by then.

"Now, I promised my lovely wife I wouldn't be long-winded," Uncle Mick said, "but I wanted to say that I have had the honor of the friendship, respect, and love of this man, and to me that is worth more than anything in this world."

Throughout the service, Mama looked around as if she was sure this was all a bad dream. I had the same feeling. I hoped Papa would surprise us by coming through the door, alive.

I'd never seen Mama look so lost. Papa had been her strength. All those years, I'd thought she was the strong one. He'd loved her enough to make her seem that way. That was true love.

Mama had once said she'd love Papa all of her days until the end of time and then some. I decided that that was the kind of love I wanted. I wanted a man who would love me for all my days and then some.

After the service, food was served in our rose garden. As my sisters were busy with their children, I looked at the beautiful roses that were Mama's pride and joy. I felt a presence behind me, and I turned around and saw Travis Sullivan.

"Like I said, Miss Annie, anything you and your mother need, I'm willing to do it for you."

With a nod, he turned and walked away. I felt as if that would be the last time I would ever speak to him.

It was a good three months before I saw Travis again. During the cold winter, I was on my way back from town when I ran into him.

"Annie, I—" he started.

"Mr. Sullivan, I see no reason for you to speak with me. I think your family has done enough to my family."

"Annie, I had no idea Sarah was—"

"I'm sorry, Mr. Sullivan, but I feel this conversation is over."

He grabbed me by the waist and pulled me off of Snake Eyes.

"How dare you—"

"Promise you'll hear me out," he said.

I looked at him. "Give me one good reason why I should?"

"Because I love you, Annie. I have always loved you. I thought you knew that."

I hesitated before I found my words. "All I know is that my papa is dead. I find it hard to believe that you claim to love me, and yet someone in your family killed him. Who will be the next one to die, and will you still love me then?"

He sighed. "Are you going to admit you care for me?"

"Mr. Sullivan..."

"My name is Travis."

"Mr. Sullivan, I would no more admit I care—"

He stepped in closer. We were inches apart, and he looked deep into my eyes. That brief moment felt like an eternity as we stood looking at each other.

Then he said again, "Annie, admit you care for me."

CHAPTER SIXTEEN

That brief encounter opened the path to our wedding day. A simple confession broke down those shields I had put up to protect myself.

I really never stopped loving Travis. I just needed time to think after what happened to Papa.

I'd been selfish because I hadn't thought about how Travis was hurting, too. He'd lost his sister-in-law and his nephew. Slowly, we got each other through the pain. At least there was a light at the end of the tunnel: our union and our wedding.

Since I was the last of the triplets to get married, I decided to stay with Mama. Our house had so many wonderful memories, and

I couldn't just leave it. Many found it odd that I chose to stay while my sisters left, but they never understood the love I had for the farm. The place was special, and I never wanted to live anywhere else.

Being the last one to marry, I felt I had found the kind of man Mama had—one who was the love of my life and who would do anything in the world for me.

Mama had also liked Travis and knew he was a good man. She said that, of all her girls, I was the gentlest and had the most love to give. She thought Travis was perfect for me—we were both shy with a great love of animals and farms.

Since Travis was a farmer, he had no problem living on our farm. We got to keep the rose garden, which was great news because there would be no other rose garden like it.

Travis had asked me to marry him in the rose garden. He got down on one knee—oh, he was like Sir Galahad asking for the fair maiden's hand in marriage.

The invitations were sent out quickly. The rose garden was done up beautifully for the wedding. My sisters' and brothers' families all attended as well as other family members and friends from town. Uncle Mick walked me down the aisle.

I chose a simple white dress and short veil. I didn't feel it wasn't necessary to wear a formal gown, so I chose something suitable for an afternoon affair. To have a long flowing gown would have been an unnecessary expense for an afternoon wedding.

On the night before the wedding, our family ended up reminiscing about the memories of all that we'd shared in our home. Not long ago, my sisters and I had been three young girls wondering what to wear to the dance.

In the morning, Aunt Mary and Mama were in the kitchen, making breakfast. I was the first one up—which had usually been the case, even when we were younger—and made my way down the stairs. I ran into Uncle Mick.

"Good morning, princess. You're up early."

"Well, there's a lot to do."

"Is there something going on today? Gee, I wish someone would let me know these things."

"Uncle Mick! You know very well what is going on today."

Smiling, he reached over and hugged me.

"I know. It's just hard to believe all of you girls are grown up. I don't understand it—you all are getting older, but I'm still young."

"I know we spent the night remembering all the good times in this house. It's kind of sad though."

"Sad?"

"Papa is not here."

"He's here—don't worry. He'll always be here. You know he loved you and your mama more than anything in this world, and when you walk down the aisle today, he'll be there. You'll know."

Later that day, as I stood in front of the mirror for a final look, Mama walked into the room. My bridal party had gone down already and taken their places. Mama looked at me with a soft smile.

"This is such a happy day for me, Annie. My last girl getting married. I'm so happy for you."

"Mama, you knew it had to happen. Though it took me a while longer than the others. I bet you thought I would never marry."

"No, I knew it would have to be a special man to capture your heart, and Travis was that man."

I took her hand. "Oh, Mama, he is the right one for me, isn't he? It's just that I have known for so long, and I wanted to be sure. I—"

"You have done the right thing, and Travis was handpicked for you." Mama looked out the window and saw the guests sitting in the rose garden. "Well, looks like it's time for us to get ready." She gave me a hug and a peck on the cheek. "I'll see you in a bit."

As if on cue, Uncle Mick walked into the room. He smiled as Mama gave me a last hug before she left to go down to the rose garden.

"You look beautiful," Uncle Mick told me. "I'm proud to walk you down the aisle."

I kissed him on the cheek. "Thank you, Uncle Mick. I could think of no one other than Papa to give me away."

"Come, lass, let's go show you off—and you should be shown off. It's your day."

I admitted that he was right. It was my day, and no one could deny anything to a bride on her wedding day. I stopped for a moment in the hall where, as a little girl, I would sit and wait for Papa to come home from work. When he arrived, I'd sit on his lap, and he'd read me a story. Mick must have known what I was thinking about because he stepped back for a moment.

"Take all the time you need, lass. I understand."

I walked into the study and walked over to the desk. I closed my eyes and could picture Papa sitting at there, smiling up and pushing back the chair so I could climb on his lap.

As if he were in the room, I heard his voice. "Have you come for my blessing, Annie? You already know I have always thought that Travis was a good man. He will be a good husband to you and will care for you and my dear Abby."

"I know, Papa. I miss you so much…"

"And I miss you too, my little Annie. But you had better get moving. Mick is pacing the floor."

"I love you, Papa."

"I love you too, Annie."

I spoke to him, yet he was not there. I slipped back out the door. Mick was standing there, smiling.

"Did he give you his blessing?"

"How did you—"

"Honey, I know you better than you do, and this was important to you. If I know Ryan, he found a way to let you know he approved."

I gave him a kiss on the cheek. "Uncle Mick, I love you so much."

He grinned. "I love myself too, Annie."

We headed to the back door and fell into line with the wedding party.

CHAPTER SEVENTEEN

Outside, everyone was waiting for the moment when I would appear at the door to walk down the aisle. Daniel led Mama to her seat, and that was the cue for the music to start.

Meghan was the first to appear, followed by Molly and Holly. With Holly being the last to walk down the aisle all eyes were on that back door. And then it happened. I stood there a few moments with Uncle Mick at my side.

"Okay," I said, "it's time to move on."

Taking Papa's place was not easy thing for Uncle Mick, but I felt Papa was there with us as we made that special walk.

When I made my way toward Travis, I felt as though I was coming home. My chest was warm with the love I had for him and for everyone who'd come to witness our love. Who knew that true love had been under my nose all along?

Mama looked at us, smiling, with tears in her eyes. She watched me become Mrs. Travis Sullivan. As we repeated our vows and placed the rings on our fingers, the pastor looked up at the congregation.

"As Annie and Travis have pledged their love to each other before God and all here, I pronounce them man and wife."

Everyone congratulated us. The music started, and we were asked to lead the first dance. I smiled and looked up at Travis. "It's very easy. Just move the way I do. We don't have to be perfect."

"I know how to waltz, Annie. My mama taught me."

He was right. He did know how to waltz, and beautifully, too. We danced most of the afternoon and into the evening, and so many of our guests joined in on the fun.

Our wedding was truly one of the best nights of my life.

Travis and I took the train to New York for our honeymoon. The trip was a gift from my sisters. It was especially exciting for Travis, who had never been out of Fall River.

After we came back, we set up residence in the farmhouse. We moved to my brothers' room to keep the big room for guests. Under Travis's hand, the alterations and additions were done with great detail, giving the old house a homey touch.

The best news was that I was expecting. My news was received with cheers from all the members of the family. They gathered at our home for a celebration of the announcement and again for the delivery that happened some six months later. For that event, everyone wanted to be there. Why, even my brother Tom came home.

It had been many years since a child had been born into the family. The house was so full that some had to sleep in the sofa in the study. I couldn't believe I was going to bring new life into this home and to be a mama.

Aunt Mary, who had been in this very house the night I and my sisters had been born, was so excited she just kept making coffee and sandwiches for everyone. Mama was in the kitchen, baking, since she felt that with all the sandwiches Mary was making, guests would soon want dessert.

The doc was there, too, to handle the delivery, but people were starting to wonder about me since the birth was taking so long. Travis was standing in the hallway with Brax and Adam. Both men were old hats at this baby business since they had a few of their own, and they tried their best to keep Travis calm.

"Does it always take this long?" Travis asked. "I mean, it is rather a long time, isn't it?"

Adam smiled at his new brother-in-law. "When Meghan had Sarah, it seemed like it took days, but it was about ten hours. Not to mention it was in the middle of a snowstorm. I wasn't even sure I could get her to the hospital, but she got there just in time. It was an experience that I will never forget. By the time Bryan came along, I was completely calm about the whole thing."

Meghan walked up behind her husband and tapped him on the shoulder. "Excuse me. Don't listen to a word he's telling you, Travis. He was a bundle of nerves both times, and there was not one moment that I recall him being calm. Meanwhile, all I wanted was to get to the hospital to calm him down."

They all began to laugh, and the mood began to feel lighter. However, Travis only calmed down when the doctor came out of the upstairs bedroom and gave everyone the good news.

Mama had slipped out to the rose garden. She was missing Pa, and she looked at the roses sadly as she thought about him.

She looked up at the sky, and suddenly, a shooting star whisked by. She heard a voice in her ear. "Make a wish, Abby girl."

"I wish you were still here, Ryan."

"I am, Abby girl."

Ryan appeared, standing in front of her, smiling and offering his hand. He was as handsome as ever, as though he hadn't aged a day.

"Come on, Abby. Let's look at the moonlight."

"You can't be here. I mean you're... you're not here. Oh, how I've missed you."

When Uncle Mick came out, he found Mama in the garden, asleep on a bench.

"Abby, Abby, wake up."

"No, Ryan, I don't want you to go... Ryan... don't leave..."

Her eyes fluttered open, and Mick came into her view.

"What are you doing here?"

He smiled at her. "Well, I'm sorry I'm not Ryan, but I came out here to tell you that Annie had a girl."

"A baby girl. Oh, Mick. Isn't it wonderful?"

"Yes, it is wonderful. Now, why don't you join us in the house and drink a toast to the new addition in the Lochlan family?" He offered his hand to her, and she got up and walked back into the house with him.

When they entered, Mary handed each of them a glass of champagne. "Is everything all right?"

"Fine," Mama said. "I fell asleep in the rose garden."

Braxton held out his champagne glass. "I propose a toast to our lovely Annie, her husband, and their newborn daughter, Amy."

Travis saw our new girl first. Then Mama came up when everyone was celebrating. She hadn't been right since Papa's death. I hoped the addition to our family would cheer her up.

She came into my room and found a tired old me, holding my new darling little Amy.

"Hi, Mama. Here she is. I hope you like the name."

Abby took the baby in her arms and smiled down at the precious little girl with the brown hair and deep-blue eyes. "Oh, I think the name is perfect. And she's perfect."

The days grew into years, and I had another child when Amy was three. Before Mama passed on to join Papa, she had the pleasure of seeing my two children grow to the ages of twelve and nine.

Mama had been ready to "go home," as she called it. The love of her life was over there, and she missed him so. She passed away quietly in the garden where she'd loved to sit at the end of each day. She'd often said she spoke to Papa out there.

That day, I'd seen her go out there and promised I would call her when supper was ready. When I was done cooking, I told Travis to get her.

He came in alone. I asked, "Is Mama coming to supper?"

"She's not coming in, Annie."

"I told her supper would be ready."

"Annie, Mama is not ever coming in again."

"What are you—"

Then it hit me what he was trying to say. "Don't leave her out there. Please bring her in, and place her in her room."

Once again, Mr. Loring was summoned to our home, and the family gathered in sorrow at yet another passing.

Aunt Mary was hit the hardest since she was now the only sister left of the original McVinny girls. As she and Uncle Mick stood at the family cemetery over the mound of trees past the rose garden, she broke down and cried.

My brothers and sisters were all in sorrow, too. The citizens of Fall River shared our grief. So many offered their condolences.

Aunt Mary delivered the eulogy at the funeral. It took her four hours to get it just right.

"Abby was my big sister, and she never let me forget it. She took over when our mother passed, and there was nothing she wouldn't do for either me or my sister Jenny. She was Papa's favorite and kept all of us together in those trying times. When she found Ryan, well, we all knew he was perfect for her, not to mention he was about the handsomest man any of us girls had ever seen."

She turned to look at her husband and smiled. "Sorry, dear, but we didn't see you till later. Anyway, as I said, they were a perfect match. Abby never stopped being a mother. First it was to me, then to her children. My sister Abby never did things easy.

"When she first told us she was having a baby, we were all excited. After all, it would mean I was going to be an aunt and not the baby of the family. Well, like I said she never did anything easy. She didn't just have one baby—she had three girls all at once. And each one was special in every way. Molly, Meghan, and Annie—and then the twin boys, Daniel and Tom—you all were so special to your mother, and she loved you each in a special way.

"So, today we are saddened by the passing of our dear Abby, yes, but we also know that she is happy that she's not only reunited with her Ryan but also her parents and two sisters." She took a pause as tears came to her eyes. "We miss you, Abby, and will hold only fond memories of you always. Until we meet again, Abby. Until we meet again."

Mary placed a rose on the coffin as Mick helped her back to one of the chairs. Then I and the rest of Ma's children and grandchildren all placed roses on the coffin.

As years passed, I too began to find the peace and tranquility of the rose garden. I now knew what Mama had felt.

I would sit in the rose garden and enjoy the night sky and watch the clouds dancing across the moon. I realized why Mama would say it was a gypsy dancing in the moonlight. At times I even felt she was dancing there for me.

Our children had grown. Amy had decided she wanted to be a teacher like me. The schoolhouse was no longer one room but had enough rooms to separate the younger ones from the older ones. Amy loved the younger ones and taught that class.

Everything had changed, yet there in the rose garden, everything was just a memory away, ready to be brought out when I wanted it. Mama had been gone ten years. We'd found her sitting there with a smile on her face. I knew she had gone with Papa. She'd always said he would come and get her when her time came. That was fitting since their love was the kind we could only find in books, the kind dreams were made out of.

I was sad that she was gone. I missed watching the moonlight with her, the advice she gave, and most of all, her love, but I knew that she was with him and my grandparents and aunts, so she wasn't alone. I found comfort in knowing that she and Papa were together, and I thought of them often when I looked up at the moon at night.

Travis sat with me every night, and we enjoyed our moments of tranquility together. He would put his arms around me and hug me tight and we'd count our blessings, grateful for the love we had for each other.

In Travis, I'd found the love I'd always dreamed of in storybooks, and we would be together until the end of our days.

ABOUT THE AUTHOR

Chloe Emile writes sweet, clean romance, whether it's contemporary or historical. She can usually be found working on her next novel, eating takeout with her husband, or watching rom-coms.

www. ChloeEmile.com